The Adventures of Huckleberry Finn

Library of Congress Cataloging-in-Publication Data

Gise, Joanne.
  Adventures of Huckleberry Finn / Mark Twain; retold by Joanne
Gise; illustrated by Ray Burns.
      p.   cm.—(Troll illustrated classics)
  Summary: The adventures of a boy and a runaway slave as they float
down the Mississippi on a raft.
    ISBN 0-8167-1857-1 (lib. bdg.)   ISBN 0-8167-7475-7 (pbk.)
    [1. Mississippi River—Fiction.   2. Missouri—Fiction.]
  I. Burns, Raymond, 1924–   , ill.   II. Twain, Mark, 1835–1910.
  Adventures of Huckleberry Finn.   III. Title.
  PZ7.G446Ad   1990
  [Fic]—dc20   89-20353

This edition published in 2002.

Copyright © 1990 by Troll Communications L.L.C.

Printed in the United States of America.

10 9 8 7 6 5

The Adventures of Huckleberry Finn

MARK TWAIN

Retold by
Joanne Gise

Illustrated by
Ray Burns

You don't know about me unless you have read a book by the name of *The Adventures of Tom Sawyer*, but that's no matter. That book was made by Mr. Mark Twain, and he told the truth, mainly.

Now the way the book winds up is this: Tom and I found the money that the robbers hid in the cave, and it made us rich. We got six thousand dollars each—all gold. It was an awful sight of money when it was piled up. Judge Thatcher took it and invested it for us. The Widow Douglas took me in as her son and said she would civilize me.

But it was rough living in her house. She made me wear new clothes that made me sweat and feel all closed in. And she was always making up rules for me to follow and telling me what bad habits I had.

Her sister, Miss Watson, had just come to live with her. She came after me with a spelling book and worked me hard. I couldn't stand it. Miss Watson would say, "Don't put your feet up there, Huckleberry," and "Don't scrunch up like that, Huckleberry. Sit up straight," and "Why don't you try to behave?"

But after three or four months had gone by, I got so I could stand it. I even went to school and could spell and read and write a little, although I wasn't much good at arithmetic. The widow said I was coming along.

One morning, I went down to the front garden. There was an inch of new snow on the ground, and I saw somebody's tracks. They had stood around the gate for a while, then went on around the garden fence. I was going to follow them. Then I noticed one of the tracks showed a cross made of nails in the left boot. Those were my father's tracks! If he was around, that meant only one thing for me—trouble!

I was down the hill in a second. I looked over my shoulder every now and then, but I didn't see anybody. I was at Judge Thatcher's as quick as I could get there.

"Why, you're all out of breath," he said to me. "Did you come for some of your money?"

"No, sir," I said. "I don't want it, not any of it. I want you to take it. I want to give you the whole six thousand."

He looked surprised. "What do you mean?" he asked.

"Don't ask me any questions," I said. "Please take it, and don't ask me anything. Then I won't have to lie."

"Is something the matter?"

"Please, sir, just take it."

He thought for a while. Then he said, "Oh, I see. You want to sell your property to me." He wrote something on a piece of paper. "This says I've bought it from you and will pay you for it. Now you sign it." I did, and then I left.

Nothing happened all that day. But when I lit my candle and went up to my room that night, there sat Pap himself!

I stood looking at him and he sat looking at me. I noticed the window was up, so he had come in by climbing from the shed roof. By and by, he said, "Fancy clothes. You think you're a big shot now, don't you?"

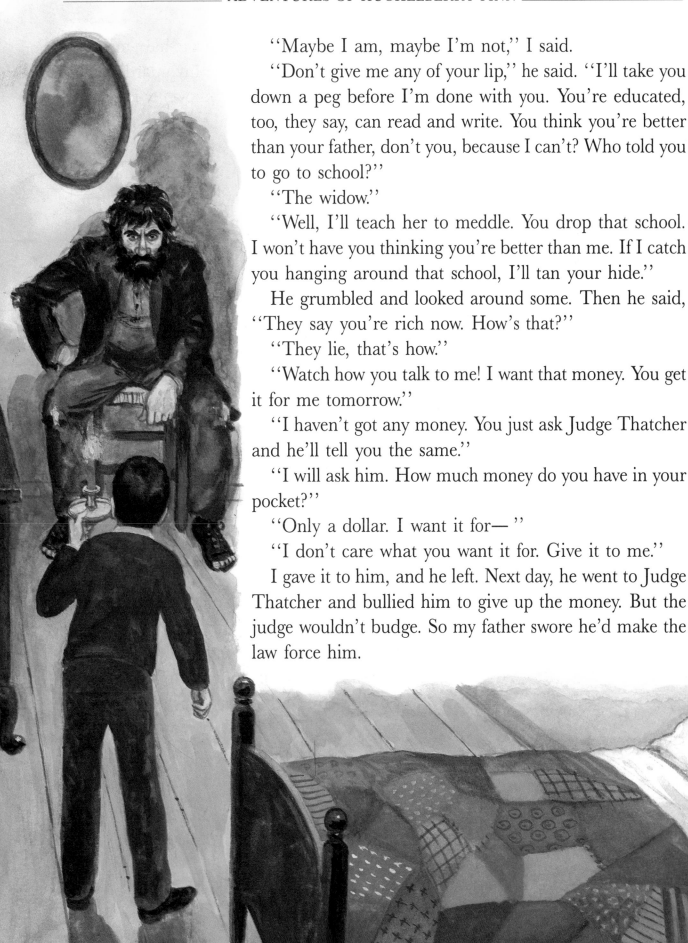

"Maybe I am, maybe I'm not," I said.

"Don't give me any of your lip," he said. "I'll take you down a peg before I'm done with you. You're educated, too, they say, can read and write. You think you're better than your father, don't you, because I can't? Who told you to go to school?"

"The widow."

"Well, I'll teach her to meddle. You drop that school. I won't have you thinking you're better than me. If I catch you hanging around that school, I'll tan your hide."

He grumbled and looked around some. Then he said, "They say you're rich now. How's that?"

"They lie, that's how."

"Watch how you talk to me! I want that money. You get it for me tomorrow."

"I haven't got any money. You just ask Judge Thatcher and he'll tell you the same."

"I will ask him. How much money do you have in your pocket?"

"Only a dollar. I want it for— "

"I don't care what you want it for. Give it to me."

I gave it to him, and he left. Next day, he went to Judge Thatcher and bullied him to give up the money. But the judge wouldn't budge. So my father swore he'd make the law force him.

The judge and the widow went to court to have me taken away from Pap and let one of them be my guardian. But the judge was new in town and didn't know my father. He said the court shouldn't separate families and that I had to stay with my father.

It seemed to take forever for the trial over my money to come up. Pap hung around the widow's house so much that she told him to quit. Well, wasn't he mad? He said he would show her who was boss.

So he watched for me, and one day he grabbed me and took me up the river about three miles. We crossed over to the Illinois shore where there were lots of woods. There weren't any houses except for an old log hut so far back in the woods that you couldn't find it if you didn't know it was there.

He kept me with him all the time, and I never got the chance to run off. We fished and hunted and things were pretty lazy and jolly.

Two months or more went by, and my clothes got to be all rags and dirt. I didn't see how I ever managed at the widow's, what with all her rules. I didn't want to go back there anymore.

But Pap beat me so much that I couldn't stand to stay with him. Plus, whenever he went to town, he would lock me up in the house. Once he was gone for three days and I got mighty lonesome. So I made up my mind to leave.

There wasn't a window in the cabin big enough to fit a dog through, and the chimney was too narrow for me. The door was made of thick oak slabs and Pap always kept the key, so I couldn't get out that way.

Then I found a rusty old saw without a handle. There was a spot at the far end of the cabin where an old blanket was nailed to keep the wind from blowing in. I lifted it up and went to work sawing out a big piece of the bottom log—big enough for me to slip through. I was nearly done when I heard Pap coming up the path. I covered up my work and hid the saw before Pap came in.

I thought I might leave while Pap was sleeping. But he slept uneasy that night. I was afraid he might wake up and catch me.

The next morning the river had begun to rise. All kinds of things were floating along. I told Pap I would check our fishing lines and walked along the bank to see what I could find.

Pretty soon, along came a beauty of a canoe. I dove into the water, climbed in, and paddled ashore. Pap hadn't seen me, so I took the canoe into a gully and hid it.

9

Pap and I pulled lots of wood out of the river that day, and even a big piece of a log raft. Pap decided to take all of it over to town and sell it. He locked me in the cabin and started off.

I had come up with a plan to make sure Pap and the widow wouldn't follow me. After I finished sawing my way out of the cabin, I took all the food, a gun, the skillet, a cup, matches, two blankets—anything I could find. I loaded everything into the canoe.

Then I put the log back in place and fixed it so no one could tell it had been sawed. I took the gun and went into the woods until I saw a wild pig. I shot it and brought it back to the cabin. I spread the pig's blood all over the inside of the house, then dumped the pig's body into the river. Finally, I took the axe from the woodpile, put some blood on it, and threw it into the corner of the house. Now it looked like someone had robbed the house and killed me.

It was about dark when I got into the canoe and sailed her down the river. I paddled to Jackson's Island. That's a place on the river where nobody lives. Tom Sawyer and Joe Harper and I had been pirates there once, so I knew all about it. Once I got there, I hid the canoe and settled down for a nap. I didn't wake up until late the next morning.

The next three days and nights passed quietly. I had seen the townsfolk dragging the river for my body, so I knew I was all right. No one would look for me anymore.

I went for a walk in the deep woods until I wasn't far from the foot of the island. All of a sudden, I walked right onto the ashes of a campfire that was still smoking!

My heart jumped up into my throat. I ran back to my camp as quick as I could and hid out there all day. I couldn't sleep much that night.

Finally, I couldn't stand it anymore. I had to find out who was on the island with me. So I got out the canoe and slipped along the shore. The moon was shining, and outside of the shadows it was almost as light as day.

When I got to the foot of the island, I pulled the canoe up to the shore, got my gun, and stepped into the woods. I could see a fire through the trees. I went up to it, careful and slow.

There was a man lying on the ground. I hid behind a clump of bushes and kept my eyes on him. Pretty soon, he woke up and stretched and threw back the blanket. It was Miss Watson's slave, Jim!

"Hello, Jim!" I shouted and jumped out of the bushes. I was awfully glad to see him. It was pretty lonesome being on the island by myself.

Jim stared at me. "Don't hurt me," he said. "I've never done anything to you. You get back in the river where you belong and don't bother me."

I wasn't long in making him see that I wasn't a ghost and I hadn't died. We had breakfast together. I asked him, "How do you come to be here, Jim?"

He looked mighty uneasy. "Maybe I shouldn't tell," he said after a moment's silence.

"Why not?"

"All right then. Huck, I've run away. Miss Watson treats me pretty rough, you know, but she always promised she wouldn't sell me down to New Orleans. But lately, there's been a slave trader around the place. Well, one night, the door was partway open, and I heard her tell the widow she was going to sell me down to Orleans for eight hundred dollars. She said she didn't want to, but she just couldn't resist that much money. I never waited to hear the rest. I took off quick, let me tell you."

Jim went on to tell how he knew they'd get dogs to track him if he stayed on land. He got into the river and held onto the back of a raft. But the man on the raft had started walking toward him with a lantern, so Jim had to let go. He swam the rest of the way to the island.

It was much nicer being on the island with Jim there. Daytimes we paddled around the island and explored everywhere. The river kept rising and rising. One night, we caught a big section of a lumber raft. It was twelve feet wide and about fifteen feet long.

Another night, we saw a house floating along. We paddled out and climbed in an upstairs window. We could see a bed and a table and two old chairs thrown around the floor. There was something lying on the floor in the far corner that looked like a man. Jim and I both hollered at him, but he didn't answer.

Finally, Jim said, "That man isn't asleep. He's dead. You stay here. I'll go see."

He went and looked. "He's been shot in the back," he said. "Come over, Huck, but don't look at his face. It's too awful."

Jim threw some rags over the man's face, but he didn't have to. I didn't want to look at a dead man. We found lots of clothes hanging on the wall. We put them all into the canoe. You never know when they might come in handy. We also got an old lantern, a butcher knife, lots of candles, a blanket, a hatchet, some nails, and a fishing line with hooks. All around, we made a good haul.

Life was fine on Jackson's Island, but we couldn't stay there. I had gone over to town one night, wearing some of the clothes we found in the house so no one would know me. I heard talk of men going to search the island for Jim.

Once I heard that, I got back to Jackson's Island as quick as I could. Jim and I got everything on the raft and into the water so fast I hardly had time to think. The raft seemed to go awfully slow, but by and by we were far enough down the river that I stopped worrying.

We tied up on shore and slept each day, and only poked our heads out when it was getting dark. At night, we sailed, caught fish, and talked—but not much. It was kind of solemn, drifting along the big, still river, lying on our backs looking up at the stars. Somehow, we just never felt like talking.

Every night we passed towns, some just a few specks of light on a hill. The fifth night we passed St. Louis, and it was like the whole world lit up. I had heard there were twenty or thirty thousand people in St. Louis, but I never believed it until I saw that wonderful spread of lights in that still night.

We said there wasn't any home like a raft. Other places seem so cramped and smothery, but a raft doesn't. You feel mighty free and easy on a raft.

 One morning, about daybreak, I took the canoe and went over to the main shore to look for some berries. Just as I was passing a place where there was a little path, I saw a couple of men running toward me as fast as they could. They yelled out that they were in trouble and being chased by men and dogs.

"All right, I'll help you," I said. "Walk up the bank a little ways, then get in the water and wade down to me and get in the canoe. That will throw the dogs off the scent."

They did as I told them. As soon as they were aboard, I paddled to the raft. I could hear men shouting and dogs barking behind us, but we were far enough away that they couldn't see us.

We all settled down to breakfast. It turned out that these two men had never met each other before. The younger man had been selling a medicine that didn't work the way he claimed it did. When the people found out, they ran him out of town. The older man was in the same kind of situation. The two decided they had a lot in common, and should work as a team.

Suddenly, the younger man said, "Friends, I trust you. So I will tell you the secret of my birth. I am really a duke! My great-grandfather was the oldest son of the Duke of Bridgewater. He came to this country, married, and died here. He left a baby son behind. That baby was cheated out of his inheritance by his uncle back in England. That infant was my grandfather. I am the rightful Duke of Bridgewater!"

Jim and I felt awfully sorry for him. We tried to make him feel better, but he said the only thing we could do was treat him like a duke. He said we had to call him "Your Grace" or "My Lord" and bow when we spoke to him. One of us should wait on him at dinner.

All that seemed easy enough, so we did it. But the old man seemed uncomfortable. "Look here," he finally said to the duke. "I'm sorry for you. But you aren't the only person who's had troubles. You aren't the only person who has a secret."

"Tell me," the duke said.

"I am the missing son of Louis the Sixteenth of France!"

You can bet Jim and I stared that time. The old man was a king!

The king said he would feel more like himself if we treated him like a king. We had to go down on one knee when we spoke to him and call him "Your Majesty" and wait on him at meals and such. So we did, and it didn't bother us much. But the duke was looking pretty unhappy.

It didn't take me long to figure out that those two weren't royalty at all, just low-down liars. But I never said a word. I didn't want any quarrels or trouble.

The four of us sailed on down the river. One day, we spotted a young man sitting on a log with two big suitcases beside him. The king told me to steer the raft toward shore. "Where are you headed?" he called to the young man.

"For the steamboat. I'm going to New Orleans."

"Get on board and we'll take you to her," the king told him.

The young man was mighty thankful. Then he said to the king, "When I first saw you, I thought you were Mr. Harvey Wilks."

"No, my name's Blodgett. Who is Mr. Wilks?"

"Peter Wilks and his brother George came here from England, leaving two other brothers behind—Harvey and William, a deaf-mute. Peter just died, and George and his wife died last year. Before Peter died, a message was sent to Harvey and William, hoping they could get here in time. The brothers hadn't seen each other since they were boys. But it's too late now. At least Harvey will get the letter, if he ever arrives."

"What letter?"

"Peter left Harvey a letter. It says where all his money is hidden and tells how to divide up the property so George's three girls will be taken care of."

The king went on asking questions and the young man told him all kinds of things. I never saw anyone who chattered on as much as that young man did.

After we'd dropped him off at the boat, the king and the duke changed into good clothes. The king was practicing talking in an English accent. I knew what he was up to, especially when he asked the duke if he could play a deaf-mute.

Then we hid the raft. Jim would have to stay with her. We hailed a boat that was coming down the river. We got off at the town about five miles down the river.

About two dozen men gathered when they saw us getting off the boat. The king asked them where Peter Wilks lived.

"I'm sorry, sir," one of them said in a gentle voice, "but he died yesterday evening."

Then the king started in crying and wailing. "Our poor brother gone, and we never got to see him!" he sobbed. Then he made all kinds of signs with his hands to the duke, and *he* started to cry. I never saw anything like it. It was enough to make me ashamed of the human race.

The news was all over town in a few minutes. Pretty soon, a big crowd escorted us to Peter Wilks' house. George's three girls, Mary Jane, Susan, and Joanna, were standing in the doorway. Their faces lit up when they saw their uncles.

We all went in the house. There was the coffin in the front room. The king and the duke went over to it, and the crowd fell back. They knelt down beside the coffin and cried some more. It was disgusting.

Everyone believed that the king and the duke were really the brothers of the dead man—everyone but the town doctor. He tried to get the others to see that they were frauds, but no one would believe him.

After a while, Mary Jane fetched Peter Wilks' letter and the king read it out loud. It left the house and three thousand dollars in gold to the girls. Peter's business and some other houses and land were given to Harvey and William, along with six thousand dollars hidden in the cellar.

The king and the duke and I went down to the cellar to get the money. When they found the bag, they spilled it out on the floor. It was a lovely sight, all of that yellow gold. You should have seen the way the king's eyes shone!

That night, we had a big supper. I really liked these people, and I was starting to feel mighty bad about how the king and the duke were planning to rob them. As the evening went by, I got to feeling worse and worse. Finally, I made up my mind to steal that bag of gold, give it back to the girls, and tell them what was going on.

Mary Jane showed us all where we would sleep. There was a cubby in the attic for me and a small guest room for the duke. She gave her own room to the king.

After supper, I said I was going up to the attic to sleep. But where I really went was to search the rooms for the gold. I figured the king would keep the money, so I looked all around his room. But I didn't dare light a candle, so it was hard to see. Then I heard footsteps coming down the hall. I ducked behind a row of dresses hanging on the wall and stood there as still as a statue.

The duke and the king came in and got to talking about what a good thing they had going here. They were going to auction off the rest of the property quickly and take the money. Then the duke said, ''I don't think we put the money in a good place. If one of the slaves finds it, he'll probably steal it.''

''You're right,'' said the king. He walked over to where I was hidden and reached in. His hand was right beside my head!

I was shaking so hard I could hardly stand it. What if the king caught me hiding there? What would he do to me?

I kept as still as I could. The king pulled the money bag out and backed away. He never knew how close he was to touching me!

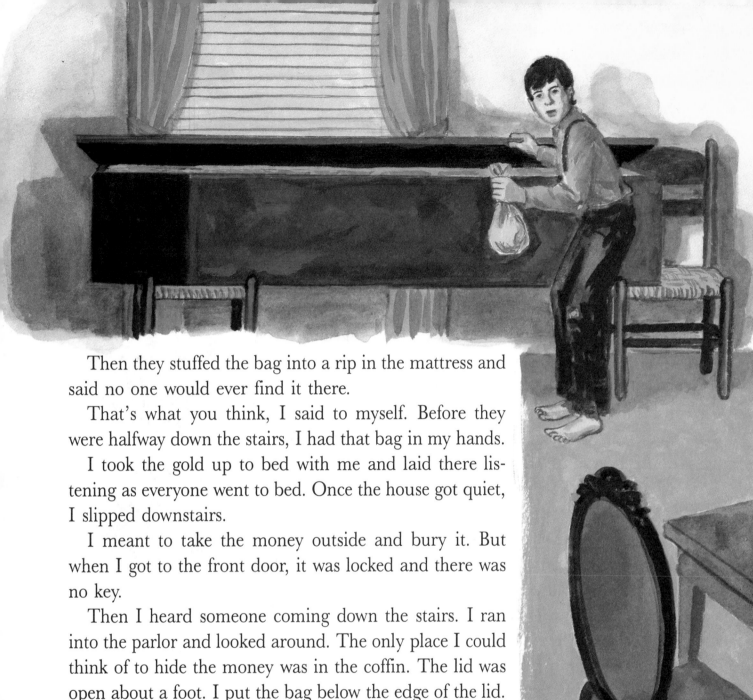

Then they stuffed the bag into a rip in the mattress and said no one would ever find it there.

That's what you think, I said to myself. Before they were halfway down the stairs, I had that bag in my hands.

I took the gold up to bed with me and laid there listening as everyone went to bed. Once the house got quiet, I slipped downstairs.

I meant to take the money outside and bury it. But when I got to the front door, it was locked and there was no key.

Then I heard someone coming down the stairs. I ran into the parlor and looked around. The only place I could think of to hide the money was in the coffin. The lid was open about a foot. I put the bag below the edge of the lid. Then I hid behind the door until the footsteps passed and it was safe to go back upstairs.

Things hadn't worked out right at all. It wouldn't be so bad if the money stayed in the coffin. I could always write Mary Jane a letter when we had gotten down the river a ways and tell her where it was. But the money was likely to be found when the coffin was closed. Then the king would get it back, and we'd be right back where we'd started. And what if someone found the money before the funeral and took it for themselves? I didn't sleep much that night.

The funeral was very long and boring. Finally, the undertaker went to close the coffin. I held my breath, certain he would look and find the money. But he just slid the lid up and screwed it shut. I didn't even know whether the money was still there or not. Now what would I write to Mary Jane? Things were getting worse all the time.

The king said he had to be getting back to England. The girls would go with him. They were so excited they didn't even seem to mind that the house and the slaves would all be sold the next day.

When the slaves were sold, the family was split up. The sons went to Memphis and the mother to New Orleans. You should have seen those girls and the slaves crying over one another. If I hadn't known the sale wasn't valid, I would have spoken up right then.

The next day, the king and the duke woke me up. "Were you in my room the other night?" the king asked me.

"No, Your Majesty."

"Have you seen anyone else go in there?"

I saw a way to take the blame for the missing money off me and put it where it wouldn't hurt anybody. "I saw some of the slaves go in there," I said.

"Well, that explains it!" the duke said. "Didn't I tell you that you can't trust those slaves with anything? Now they're gone, and we'll never get our money back."

Then he and the duke went downstairs. I went down, too. I saw Mary Jane crying. She felt bad about selling the slaves and splitting up their family. "I never thought that would happen," she said. "Just think, that family will never see each other again."

"But they will. They'll be together again within two weeks," I blurted out without thinking. Then I was stuck. I thought about it for a while, then decided that the best thing to do would be to tell the truth.

So I told Mary Jane the whole story. She was angry, of course, and wanted to have the king and the duke run out of town.

"No," I said, thinking of Jim waiting on the raft. "Don't do that. You see, there's someone else involved, and he'll be in danger if these rascals find out I've told on them. I'll tell you what to do. Do you have a friend you could stay with till about half past nine tonight?"

"Yes."

"Go there, then, and don't say a word about this. When you get back tonight, I'll be gone, and my friend with me. Then you can tell everyone in town that these two are frauds. The doctor thinks that already, so he'll help you. Will you do that?"

"Of course." Then she took my hand and her eyes were full of tears. "Goodbye," she said. "I'll never forget you." Then she left. I never saw her again, but many's the time I've thought of her. She was the best girl I ever knew.

The auction of Peter Wilks' property was held that afternoon. It dragged on and on. Pretty near everything had been sold when a steamboat landed at the dock.

Pretty soon, a crowd came running up, hollering and laughing. "Here's another set of heirs to Peter Wilks!" they shouted. "Now, which are the real ones?"

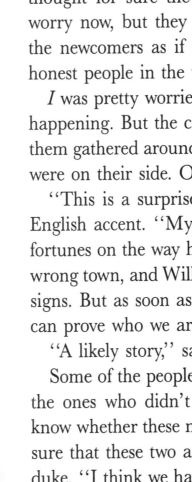

There were two gentlemen with them, one older and one young. The younger man had his arm in a sling. I thought for sure the king and the duke would have to worry now, but they didn't. Instead, they just looked at the newcomers as if they couldn't bear to see such dishonest people in the world.

I was pretty worried though—I hadn't counted on this happening. But the crowd thought it was funny. Some of them gathered around the king and the duke to show they were on their side. Others sided with the newcomers.

"This is a surprise to me," said the older man in an English accent. "My brother and I have had some misfortunes on the way here. Our baggage was put off at the wrong town, and William broke his arm, so he can't make signs. But as soon as our baggage arrives, I assure you I can prove who we are."

"A likely story," said the king, laughing.

Some of the people agreed, but not all of them. One of the ones who didn't was the doctor. He said, "I don't know whether these newcomers are frauds, but I know for sure that these two are." He pointed to the king and the duke. "I think we have to make sure they don't get away. Let's bring all four of these men to the tavern and question them."

So the crowd led us along. I had to go, too. We sat in the tavern for hours. First the king had to tell his story. Then the newcomer told his. They even asked me questions. The king gave me a look, so I had to lie. I guess I wasn't very good at it, because everyone laughed at me.

The doctor wanted the king to give him the bag of gold for safekeeping. The king told him the slaves had stolen it. I don't think the doctor believed him, but he didn't say anything.

Then the new man said, "I've just thought of something that might settle this. Is there anyone here who laid out Peter's body?"

"I did," someone said.

"Then perhaps this other person can tell us what was tattooed on Peter's chest?"

Well, the king wasn't expecting that! How would he know what was tattooed on the man? Now he'll have to give up, I said to myself. But I was wrong!

"Yes, I can tell you," the king said. "It's a small, thin, blue arrow. It's so faint it's hard to see unless you look close."

"No," said the newcomer. "What you saw were Peter's three initials, P-B-W. Isn't that right?"

"No. I didn't see any mark at all."

Everyone started yelling then, saying that all of them were frauds. Then, a lawyer jumped up and shouted, "There's only one thing to do. We'll dig up the body and look for ourselves."

Everyone liked that idea. "We'll do it," they said. "And if we don't find any tattoos, we'll hang the lot of them!"

I was really scared now. I'd never been in this much trouble in my life.

When we got to the graveyard, everyone swarmed over the grave and started to dig. At last, they got the coffin out and unscrewed the lid. Then someone yelled, "Here's the bag of gold on his chest!"

The man who was holding my wrist got so excited he let go of me and pushed forward to have a look. I ran away from there so fast, no one even saw me.

I flew through town as fast as my feet would take me. When I was out of town, I found a boat and borrowed it. I paddled as hard as I could to get where the raft was hidden. Then I jumped on board and shouted, "Let's go, Jim! Set her loose! Glory be, we're done with them!"

In two seconds we were floating down the river. It felt so good to be free again I just had to jump in the air for joy.

But my happiness didn't last long. I heard a boat coming up behind us. And when I looked, there were the king and the duke paddling a canoe after us. We weren't done with them after all. It was all I could do to keep from crying.

The king was furious with me, but I told him that the man who had hold of me had told me to run away so I wouldn't get hung. And I said both Jim and I were awfully glad to see them again. This calmed the king down some, though he was still pretty mad. It turned out they had gotten away the same way I had.

We sailed down the river for days and days. We didn't dare stop at any towns along the way. We were way down south now, and a long way from home. We began to see trees with Spanish moss hanging from the limbs like long, gray beards. It made the woods look spooky.

The king and the duke spent the time whispering together. I didn't like it, and neither did Jim. We knew they were up to something.

One morning, we hid Jim and the raft in a safe place and the king went into a village. After a while, the duke and I went to meet him. I knew the king was up to some mischief. If only I could get away from them!

Luck was with me. Those two rascals got into an argument with some of the village folk. They took no notice of me. I took off down the road like a deer.

When I got near where we'd hidden the raft, I shouted, "Set her loose, Jim! We're all right now!" But there was no answer. And when I got to the raft, Jim was gone!

I sat there for a while, feeling sad and scared. Finally, I went back to the road. I met a boy and asked him if he'd seen anyone who looked like Jim.

"Yes," he said. "He's at Silas Phelps' place two miles below here. He's a runaway slave, you know."

"Really?" I said. "How did Mr. Phelps catch him?"

"A stranger sold him to Mr. Phelps for forty dollars. The stranger said there's a two hundred dollar reward down New Orleans way for this slave, but he didn't have time to go south and collect it. So he sold the slave to Mr. Phelps." He went on to describe the stranger, and blamed if it wasn't the king! That scoundrel!

Finally, it came to me that the only thing to do was steal Jim out of slavery. So I started down the road to the Phelps' house.

I didn't have any particular plan. I just walked into the yard, hoping things would work out somehow. And they did—kind of.

A woman came running out of the house, followed by a couple of children. She was all excited. "It's you at last!" she shouted and hugged me tight. "I'm so glad to see you after all these years! Children, say hello to your cousin, Tom."

I was really up a stump now. Before I could say anything, the woman—she told me to call her Aunt Sally—had led me into the house and was asking so many questions I couldn't manage to get the truth out at all. I told her I had gotten off the steamboat a little ways up the river, hid my baggage, and walked down.

"Your Uncle Silas went to town to look for you," Aunt Sally told me. "Here he comes now. Let's play a little joke on him." She led me behind the bed and told me to crouch down so I was hidden.

An old man came in. Aunt Sally asked, "Has he come?"

"No," said her husband.

"Oh, dear, where can he be?" Aunt Sally said, looking upset. Then, "Look outside, Silas," she said. As soon as he'd turned around, she motioned to me to come out of my hiding place. When Silas saw me, he said, "Who's that?"

"Why, Silas, who do you think it is? It's Tom Sawyer!"

Well, you can believe I nearly fell through the floor. But then I relaxed a little. At least I could talk about Tom and his family. And that's just what happened. All Sally and Silas could do was ask me questions about Tom's cousin Mary and his half-brother Sid and his Aunt Polly. It turned out Aunt Polly was Aunt Sally's sister.

I was chattering away when suddenly I heard the steamboat whistle. What if Tom's on that boat? I thought. What if he comes here and calls me by name? I couldn't let that happen, so I told the folks I would go fetch my baggage. Silas said I could take the horse and wagon.

I was halfway to town when I saw another wagon heading toward me. Sure enough, it was Tom Sawyer. I stopped and waited for him.

Tom's mouth fell open when he saw me and he looked scared to death. "I never did anything to you," he said at last. "What do you want to come back and haunt me for?"

"I haven't come back," I said. "I've never been gone."

"You're not a ghost?"

"No. I wasn't murdered at all. I played a trick on everyone to get away from my father."

That satisfied him. Then I had to tell him all about my adventures rafting down the river. Tom thought that was grand. But then I told him the fix I was in now, what with Jim being captured and Tom's family thinking I was him.

"We can fix that," Tom said. "You take my trunk and go back to the house. I'll come along a little after you. Don't let on that you know me at first, all right?" I agreed. Tom always had a good plan in his head.

"As for Jim, he's—" Tom started to say. Then he stopped and got a funny look on his face. "I'll help you steal him!" he said suddenly.

So we settled on everything and I started back to the house. I'd been back about half an hour when Tom's wagon drove into the yard.

"Who could that be?" Aunt Sally said. "It must be a stranger passing through. We'll have to put on another plate for dinner."

Tom came in and spun a big story about how he was from Ohio and he was on his way to visit a family in the next town. He went on and on so that I started to get nervous and wonder how he was going to help me.

All of a sudden, he leaned over and kissed Aunt Sally right on the mouth!

She jumped up and screamed at him. Tom looked hurt and surprised. "I'm sorry, ma'am," he said. "I thought you'd like it. They told me to kiss you. They said you'd like it."

"Who said that?"

"Why, everybody." He looked at me. "Tom, didn't you think Aunt Sally would be happy to have a kiss from Sid Sawyer?"

"Sid!" Aunt Sally jumped up and hugged and kissed Tom, and scolded him for fooling her. She believed he was his own half-brother!

"We didn't expect you to come," Aunt Sally said at last. "Sis only wrote me that Tom was coming."

"Tom was supposed to be the only one, but I begged and begged to go, too. At the last minute, she let me go. Coming down the river, we decided it would be a first-rate trick for Tom to come here alone and for me to follow and pretend I was a stranger."

After we finished eating, Tom and I said we were tired and went up to bed. We were to share the same bed. As soon as we got up there, we fell to talking about Jim.

"I bet I know where Jim is," Tom said. "Did you see that little cabin at the edge of the yard?" I nodded. "Well," Tom went on, "during dinner I saw a slave take some food in there. He unlocked the door when he went in and locked it when he came out. Then he brought the key back to Uncle Silas. So there's a prisoner in that cabin, and the prisoner must be Jim!"

"Let's steal the key from Uncle Silas," I said. "We'll let Jim out, take him to where I hid the raft, and sail down the river. Wouldn't that plan work?"

Tom looked disgusted. "Of course it would work! But it's too easy. What's the good of a plan that's so easy? Now, listen to *my* plan."

Tom's plan was worth fifteen of mine for style, would make Jim a free man, and might get us killed besides. It was a great plan, and I told Tom so.

Tom and I slipped out the window and down to the ground and set off in the direction of the cabin. There was a window hole in one side of the cabin. It had a board nailed across it.

"That hole's big enough for Jim to get through," I told Tom. "All we have to do is pull off the board."

"I hope we can find a way that's a little more complicated than that!" Tom said.

There was a lean-to attached to the cabin. Tom and I slipped inside. The lean-to had just a dirt floor. Tom was joyful. "Here's what we'll do!" he said. "We'll dig him out!"

The next day, Tom and I made friends with the slave who went to feed Jim. He let us go into the cabin with him. Jim was smart and didn't let on that he knew us. Tom took him aside and told him we were going to rescue him.

We set to work after everyone had gone to bed. We pretended it took thirty-seven years to dig through to Jim's cabin, but it really took only three hours.

Jim was asleep when we climbed into his cabin. We lit a candle and woke him up. He was so glad to see us he almost cried. Jim wanted to escape right away, but Tom told him to wait a bit. When the moment was right, Tom said, we'd be sure to get Jim to safety.

A couple of weeks went by. I heard that the king and the duke had tried to pull one of their tricks in the village. But the people got wise and ran them out of town. You can bet I was glad to be rid of them at last!

Uncle Silas had written a few times to the plantation Jim supposedly escaped from. But since that was a story made up by the king, no one ever answered. Finally, he decided to advertise in the New Orleans and St. Louis papers. That made me nervous, and I said we couldn't wait anymore to set Jim free.

"You're right," Tom said. "It's time for the letters."

"What letters?"

"Letters to warn people that something's going to happen."

I didn't get it.

"If we don't tell them something's up, they won't try to stop it. After all our hard work, do you want this escape to go off so easy?"

"Well, yes. I wouldn't mind that."

Tom glared at me. I quickly said, "But I won't complain. You just work things the way you think best and I'll go along."

Tom was glad to hear that. He sat right down and wrote a note that said:

Beware. Trouble is brewing. Keep a sharp lookout.

UNKNOWN FRIEND

I slipped it under the front door that night. You wouldn't believe the stir it caused. Everyone was as jumpy as a frog. Aunt Sally was the worst. If a door banged, she jumped. If anything fell, she jumped. If you happened to touch her when she didn't see you, that made her jump, too.

Then Tom wrote a letter that told how a gang from the Indian Territory was planning to steal Jim at midnight. He put it by the door. It caused even more of a fuss than the first letter. They all were in such a sweat they didn't know which end they were standing on.

Tom and I had to go to bed right after supper, but we sneaked out as soon as we could and headed down to the cellar. There was plenty of food there. We made up a good meal to take with us, and headed back upstairs. Then Tom said, "Where's the butter?"

"I laid out a hunk of it on a piece of corn bread," I said.

"Well, you must have left it downstairs. Go back down and fetch it. I'll meet you out by Jim's cabin."

38

So out he went, and I went down to the cellar. There was the hunk of butter and the corn bread where I'd left it. I picked it up and started upstairs. Then I saw Aunt Sally coming toward me! The only thing I could think to do was put the bread and butter in my hat and clap it on my head.

"What were you doing down there?" Aunt Sally asked me.

"Nothing."

"What made you go down there at this time of night?"

"I don't know."

"You don't *know*? You just march into the sitting room and sit there till I come. You've been up to something, and I'm going to find out what it is."

She went away and I opened the sitting room door. My, but there was a crowd there! Fifteen farmers, and every one of them had a gun. I was so scared I didn't know what to do. I had to get to Tom and Jim before these men went outside with their guns.

Aunt Sally came back and started to ask me questions. But I was so fidgety I couldn't answer them straight. The room was mighty hot, but I didn't dare take off my hat.

Pretty soon, I felt the butter start to melt and drip down the back of my neck. Then, a streak of it came trickling down my forehead. Aunt Sally saw it and let out a shriek. "The child's got brain fever!" she yelled. "His brains are oozing out!" She snatched off my hat, and there was the bread and butter.

Aunt Sally grabbed me and hugged me. "What a scare you gave me!" she said. "Why didn't you tell me that was why you were downstairs? I wouldn't have cared. Now go back to bed and don't let me see any more of you until morning!"

I was upstairs in a second and outside in another. I ran into the lean-to and told Tom we had to run for it now. When he heard about all the men with guns in the house, his eyes lit up. "That's wonderful! Why Huck, if we had to do it over again, I bet we could— "

"Hurry!" I interrupted him. "*Hurry!*"

But just as we were ready to leave, we heard men outside the door of the cabin. "They haven't come yet," one of them said. "The door is still locked. Some of you wait inside and kill them when they come. The rest of us will keep a lookout."

We waited until it got quiet. Then Tom and Jim and I slipped outside and headed for the fence. Jim and I got over the fence all right, but Tom's pants caught on the top rail. The wood made a noise when he pulled free— and the men heard it. They started to fire.

"Here they are! After them! Get the dogs!"

We ran into the bushes and hid. The dogs came running toward us. But they were our dogs, so they knew us and ran by us without a sound. When the men and the dogs were far enough away, Tom and Jim and I slipped over to the raft and paddled out to an island.

"Now, Jim, you're a free man!" I told him. We were all as glad as could be. Tom was the gladdest of all, because he had a bullet in his leg.

When Jim and I heard that, we didn't feel as happy as we did before. We tied the wound up with rags and made Tom lie down. Tom wanted Jim and me to sail away without him, but the wound looked bad to me. I knew Tom needed a doctor, and Jim knew it, too. He said he wouldn't leave without a doctor seeing to Tom.

Well, that made Tom plenty mad, but Jim and I wouldn't give in. I got the raft ready and left Jim and Tom in the woods while I sailed back to town to fetch a doctor.

The doctor was very kind, even when I woke him up in the middle of the night. I told a story about how my brother and I had been camping and he had shot himself by accident. The doctor didn't look like he believed me. He went, but he wouldn't let me go along. ''You go on home,'' he said. ''Your folks will be worried.''

I had no intention of going home, though. I slept the rest of the night in a lumber pile. When I woke up in the morning, I meant to go to the island and check on Tom. But no sooner had I turned the corner when I ran right into Uncle Silas!

''Tom! Where have you been all this time?''

''Hunting for the runaway slave,'' I mumbled.

''Well, you go right home. Your aunt is worried sick.''

When I got home, Aunt Sally was so glad to see me she laughed and cried all together. She wanted to know where Sid was, so I made up a story that he was around town somewhere, looking for more news of the escape.

They all believed me, but when Tom hadn't come back by supper they started worrying all over again. I felt just terrible because I couldn't tell them where Tom was and make them feel better. I couldn't even slip out that night and head back to the island. Aunt Sally had found out how we'd sneaked out the window to chase Jim and made me promise not to do it again. She was so upset, I just couldn't break that promise and hurt her anymore.

I couldn't see how I would get through the next day without any word. It turned out I didn't have to. Just after breakfast, we all saw something coming up the road. It was Tom, lying on a mattress, and the doctor, and Jim with his hands tied behind him, and a whole crowd of people following.

Aunt Sally thought Tom was dead at first, but he wasn't. He was pretty bad off, though. Aunt Sally settled him right into bed.

Jim was locked up in the cabin again. This time they set a guard on him and chained him, too. They would have done worse, but the doctor put in a good word for him. He said Jim had been a big help in nursing Tom, even though he risked his freedom by staying with him. So the people were kinder to him. But that didn't make me feel much better. Jim was still a prisoner.

Tom was better by morning. Aunt Sally and I were sitting by his bed when he woke up.

He was full of fire and wanted to talk all about our grand rescue. He went on and on to Aunt Sally, and told her all about our work and plotting to free Jim. She could hardly believe her ears. I swear, if Tom wasn't so sick, she would have thrashed him.

"Well," she said at last, "I'm glad you had such fun at our expense. If I catch you meddling with him again— "

"Meddling with who?" Tom asked.

"Why, the runaway slave, of course."

Tom's face got all serious. He said, "Didn't he get away?"

"No," Aunt Sally said. "We've got him back. He's chained so he won't get loose until he's claimed or sold."

Tom sat straight up. He looked angrier than I'd ever seen him. "You've got no right to lock him up! Set him loose! He's no slave—he's as free as you or I!"

"What are you talking about?" Aunt Sally and I asked at the same time.

"Tom and I have known Jim all our lives. Old Miss Watson died two months ago. She felt so bad about planning to sell him that she set Jim free in her will."

Aunt Sally looked puzzled. "What did you want to set him free for, if he was already free?"

"Why, I wanted the adventure of it!"

All of a sudden, Tom turned. There was Tom's Aunt Polly, standing in the doorway! Aunt Sally jumped up and hugged her almost to death. While they were carrying on, I hid under the bed.

In a little while, Aunt Polly pulled away and stared at Tom as if she were trying to grind him into the ground. He looked away. She said, "You'd better look away. I would, too, if I were you, Tom."

"Why, Sis, that's not Tom," Aunt Sally said. "It's Sid. Tom is—where is that boy? He was here a minute ago."

"You mean where's Huck Finn! Come out from under that bed, Huck."

Aunt Sally was one of the most mixed-up people I ever did see. Then Aunt Polly told her all about me.

Miss Watson really did set Jim free in her will. Aunt Polly confirmed Tom's story, and Jim was let out of the cabin. The whole family made a fuss over him then, and we all had a grand time talking.

I could hardly believe it, but after all that happened, Tom was ready for *another* adventure. He said we should all buy fancy outfits and go into Indian Territory for a week or two. But I said I couldn't. I didn't have any money, and I figured I couldn't get any from home. I'd been gone so long that Pap must have gotten hold of it and used it all up by now.

"It was all there when I left," Tom said. "Your Pap left town with some mean-looking strangers and never came back."

"He won't ever be coming back," Jim said. He looked very serious.

"Why not?"

He didn't want to tell me, but I kept at him. Finally, he said, "Do you remember that house we saw floating down the river? Do you remember there was a dead man in there, and I covered him up and wouldn't let you look at him?" I nodded, and he went on. "That was your father, Huck. He won't bother you anymore."

Tom's just about well now. He wears the bullet on a chain around his neck. So there's nothing more for me to write about. I'm glad, because if I knew how much trouble it was to make a book, I never would have started this one. Anyway, I've got to head for Indian Territory ahead of the others. Aunt Sally says she's going to adopt me and civilize me. I can't stand it. I've been there before.